SLACKSVILLE'S SILLIEST SPOOKY STORIES

TALES FROM SLACKSVILLE

K. PEACH

STRANGE GOOSE

Cover art by Andrew Dieffenbach

Design by Jonathan Hooker

Edited by Stacie Gensic

Illustrations by K. Peach

ISBN 978-1-7364426-7-8

eBook ISBN 978-1-7364426-8-5

For Jon.

I wrote this book because you encouraged me to.

INTRODUCTION

Welcome to Slacksville! The town with a factory just for slacks. The town where spooky stories are a little sillier than in other towns. The town where unusual things tend to happen because it was built in 1922 on an enormous patch of glow-in-the-dark scratch-and-sniff fungus that was exposed to radiation by a meteorite. Radioactive fungus can really make things silly and spooky.

CHAPTER ONE

The Tooth Fairy

"Mom," Trisha said, "I think you're the tooth fairy."

Trisha wiggled her sharp tooth for the fiftieth time that day. Her dad said it was "hanging on by a thread."

"What? No, I'm not the tooth fairy," her mom said while driving them home from school. "Why would you think that?"

"How does the tooth fairy get in the house?"

"Oh, that's not so difficult to understand. The fairies live in the Slacksville Forest in another dimension. They open a portal from their dimension to ours, travel through time and space, land on your bed, and climb under your pillow."

Trisha imagined a beautiful little woman with shimmering wings and braided black hair. She thought about how the fairy would appear standing on her blanket and fly to the edge of her pillow, maybe carrying a big coin.

"I want to see her," Trisha said, "I'm going to stay up and see her."

Her mother smiled.

"That's what all kids say, but they always fall asleep."

"That changes tonight," Trisha whispered to herself. She started to form a plan.

When Trisha got home, she waited for her mother to be distracted, then she took five of her dad's energy drinks from the refrigerator and a bowl of ice and hid them under her bed. Next, she set an alarm that would vibrate every ten minutes throughout the night. She tucked a washcloth away under her pillow. Finally, she had to pull out her tooth.

She tied a string around the tooth, tied the other end to a door knob, and then flung the door shut. The tooth was yanked away from her gums. She grinned a bloody grin at the tooth and placed it under her pillow.

"Trisha! Dinner!" her mom called.

Trisha washed the blood from her mouth and made sure not to smile during dinner. This lost tooth would be her little secret.

The hallway light blinked out. *Good*, Trisha thought, *Everyone is in their room now.* She yawned and began the process of staying awake. First, she took a big drink of Energy Slam. It tasted like liquid candy.

Then she dipped her washcloth in the bowl of half-melted ice and slapped herself across the face with it.

She followed the same steps every ten minutes, but soon became more and more tired...and bored. The light from her night light wasn't enough to read a book and she couldn't play music or else she might not hear the tooth fairy arriving.

I guess it wouldn't hurt to lay down while I wait, she thought.

She took another drink of Energy Slam and slapped herself across the face with a cold washcloth one more time, then laid down. Her eyes became heavier and heavier.

Thankfully, her alarm woke her back up just in time to see a shimmering at the foot of her bed. She sat up.

"Tooth Fairy? Is that you?" she whispered.

Then she nearly screamed.

She knew for sure that this must be the tooth fairy, but it wasn't a little woman. She didn't have wings or braids. She didn't wear a dress made of flower petals and she didn't smell like roses.

Instead, it was like a mass of teeth all stuck together with pink gum that was rolling, sliding, and crawling toward her like a slug. It left a trail behind it like wet oatmeal and the children's teeth were shiny with spit and yellow with grime.

Trisha tried not to be afraid. She knew it couldn't be dangerous. She *had* lost other teeth, so apparently this horrible looking tooth fairy had been in her bedroom before. It was like what her mom said about spiders–*they're more afraid of you than you are of them.*

She moved her pillow away so the fairy could reach the tooth *and* so the fairy wouldn't get slime on it. It continued to roll and crawl until it moved over the tooth, absorbed it, and released a coin.

"Can you talk?" Trisha whimpered.

"Loose teeeeeeeeeth," the fairy grunted.

"Aren't fairies supposed to be pretty and grant wishes and things?" Trisha asked.

"Rude. You bully," the fairy said.

"Sorry," Trisha said.

"Loose teeth?"

"You want more teeth? I don't have another one ready yet. This one is loose, but it's still in my mouth," Trisha said. She demonstrated by wiggling another tooth.

"Me want loose teeth!" the fairy grumbled.

Trisha backed herself against the wall.

"No! It's not ready yet!"

"LOOSE TEETH!" it grunted and began to climb up her arm.

"NO!"

The door flung open and the light came on.

"What are you doing up?" her dad asked.

Trisha looked down. The fairy was gone.

"Dad! The tooth fairy came and it was awful! It was like a little monster!"

Her dad looked at a mess on the floor.

"Are those my energy drinks?" he asked.

"Dad, aren't you listening?"

"We'll talk about this in the morning," he said. "Go back to sleep."

He shut off the light and closed the door. Trisha felt a familiar weight on her chest. In the darkness, the fairy had returned!

"LOOSE TEEEEEEEEETH!" it cried.

Trisha opened her mouth in a silent scream. The tooth fairy climbed over the edge of her bottom lip, sucked out the loose tooth, burped, and dropped out another coin. It started to crawl toward the foot of her bed once again.

Trisha put a finger in her mouth and felt a space where her other loose tooth had been.

The tooth fairy seemed to dissolve away in a shimmering cloud.

They'll see the slime the fairy left and they'll have to believe me, Trisha thought. She flicked on the light. The slime was gone. There was no trace of the tooth fairy, except for the two coins it left behind.

No one's going to believe me, Trisha thought. *Next time, I'll be ready.*

It wasn't long before Trisha had another opportunity to meet the tooth fairy and she had been planning and preparing even more than before. At first, she thought she could just take a picture of the tooth fairy, but what if some kind of magic kept the tooth fairy from appearing in photos?

There was only one way to prove she saw the tooth fairy–she had to capture it.

She had no trouble staying awake this time. When the tooth fairy appeared at the foot of her bed, she pulled an old aquarium out from under her bed, turned her blanket over, dumped the fairy in, and covered it with a lid.

"Got you!" she whispered.

She hadn't thought about what would happen next, other than maybe she'd be famous–the first person to ever capture the tooth fairy.

She also felt a little sad. Did this mean no other kids would get a mysterious visit from the tooth fairy ever again? *I'll let it go* ***after*** *I get famous*, she thought.

"Help," the fairy grunted.

"Don't be scared," Trisha said, "I'll feed you! You'll be fine."

Trisha pulled her tooth out from under her pillow and slipped it into the aquarium. The fairy consumed it and pooped out a coin.

"Help," it grunted again.

Who is it calling to for help? Trisha wondered.

It wasn't long before her question was answered. There was a shimmering at the foot of her bed again and another tooth fairy appeared.

"I didn't know there was more than one of you!" she whispered. Just before she could dump the second fairy into the aquarium with the first one, another appeared, and another, and another! Tooth fairies like slugs the size of footballs surrounded

Trisha. Each one gleamed with sharp teeth and spit. Some of them worked to remove the cover from the aquarium while others climbed Trisha's body leaving little teeth marks on her arms and cheeks.

"Mean. Bully," one of them said.

"I'm not a bully! I just wanted to use you so I could get famous!" Trisha said.

"Teeth!" it said.

"I don't have any more loose teeth!" Trisha said.

"Teeth!" it said again and began to climb onto her chin...onto her lip...into her mouth.

Trisha screamed.

The light flicked on.

"What's wrong?!" her mother cried, "Did you have a bad dream?"

Trisha looked around her. No fairies. They were all gone.

"Um. Yeah. Just a bad dream," she said, breathing fast.

Last time they reappeared when the light was turned off, she thought.

"Mom, can I sleep with the light on?" she asked.

"Sure. Good night!" her mom said.

Trisha studied the faint teeth marks on her arms.

I'm never sleeping with the lights out again.

CHAPTER TWO

Sweaty Guy

It had been a regular basketball practice at Smirk Middle School that ended with the boys filing into the boys locker room. It smelled good, as it always did–like boiled socks. Kevin couldn't help but notice how sweaty Mo was. Mo's hair was drenched and sticking to his face.

"Dude, was there a rainstorm I didn't know about?" Kevin joked.

"The curse is real," Mo mumbled.

"What? Did you say curse?" Kevin asked.

"I shouldn't have done it," Mo said as he examined the moisture on his hands.

"Just tell me what happened," Kevin said.

"My cousins were visiting. Late at night, they told me about the ghost that if you say its name in the dark in a mirror three times, the ghost curses you with 'being sweaty all the time.'"

"That sounds dumb."

"That's what I thought. I didn't think it could be real, so to try to prove it wasn't real, I did it."

"And then what happened?" Kevin asked.

"Nothing happened right away, but I woke up in the middle of the night super sweaty. I had to yank all the sheets off my bed and sleep on a towel and use another towel for a blanket. I woke up sweaty again and had to make a nest out of paper towels."

"Could it be a coincidence?" Kevin asked.

"No. I've been sweaty ever since. It's like my armpits are a faucet."

"Dude, ghosts aren't even real. There's no way *that's* the reason why you're sweaty."

"Why don't *you* do it then?" Mo challenged Kevin.

"Oooooooooooh," everyone around them said, so then Kevin *had* to do it. He rolled his eyes, sure there was nothing to it.

"Fine. But nothing's going to happen. What's the name of the ghost?"

"Sweaty Guy," Mo said.

Kevin walked over to the locker room light switch and shut it off. He could barely see the mirror with only the red light of the emergency exit sign. It cast a red glow behind his head.

"Sweaty Guy. Sweaty Guy. Sweaty Guy."

"BOO!" Davy said, jumping up behind him.

Kevin's heart leapt. He flicked the light back on and wiped at his forehead to the sound of a dozen boys laughing.

"See? No sweat."

Kevin held up his hand as evidence. Mo gasped.

"It started. Look at your armpit!"

Everyone looked at Kevin's armpit. The pit of his light gray shirt was damp and dark gray.

"Whatever," Kevin said, "That's just still from basketball practice."

Mo wiped his hands across his shirt.

"If you figure out a way to reverse the curse, let me know," Mo said. "I'm getting desperate."

Kevin felt bad for Mo. How embarrassing to be dripping sweat all over the place.

Kevin's dad picked him up from practice.

"Pee-yew!" he said when Kevin got in the car.

Kevin sniffed at his own armpit.

"That bad?"

"You better shower before dinner," his dad said.

At home, Kevin took off his shoes and noticed that his socks were wet, almost like he had stepped in a puddle.

"Yikes, I guess I do need a shower."

He showered, but the sweat kept coming. He started to worry.

At dinner he complained to his dads about it. They simply smiled at each other.

"Don't worry," they said, "It's normal. You just need to shower every morning and wear some deodorant."

Kevin wondered how he was going to hide the sweat at school the next day. He put on a tank top to stay cool, but then he could see the sweat running down his arms. He put on a thick sweatshirt to hide it, but the sweat soaked all the way through.

Resigned to his sweatiness, Kevin went into his bathroom to brush his teeth before bed. He looked in the mirror and got an idea. He flicked off the light.

"Sweaty Guy. Sweaty Guy. Sweaty Guy." He said, "Are you there? I'm sorry I bothered you. Can you stop the curse, please? I can't show up to school tomorrow like this."

A figure appeared in the mirror beside him. It was difficult to see in the darkened room, but the little light that there was reflected off of its wet skin.

"Why did you summon meeeeeee?!" Sweaty Guy howled.

"I'm sorry!" Kevin cried.

"No, I mean it, *why*? Like, what did you get out of it? You had everything to lose and nothing to gain. Honestly, boys keep telling each other stories about me and I don't know why so many of them take the risk."

"I don't know. I guess I wanted to prove you weren't real."

"How did that work out for you?" Sweaty Guy asked.

Kevin hung his head low.

"Just follow your dads' directions and I'm sure you'll be fine," Sweaty Guy said, then laughed an eerie laugh and disappeared.

Kevin tossed and turned all night on towel after towel. In the morning, he sleepily walked into the bathroom to shower. The steam filled the room and covered the mirror with fog. That's when Kevin saw it.

"Yug Ytaews?"

It was written three times on the mirror.

"Oh! It's Sweaty Guy! It says Sweaty Guy backwards! Thanks, Sweaty Guy!"

The light was dim enough that Sweaty Guy appeared.

"Oh, shoot," Kevin said, "I accidentally said your name three times. Sorry."

Sweaty Guy rolled his eyes and disappeared again.

"OK, here goes nothing," Kevin said, "Yug Ee-teh-wus, Yug Ee-teh-wus, Yug Ee-teh-wus. Am I forgetting something? Is it that easy?"

He stopped sweating immediately.

At school he ran to Mo to tell him the cure.

"Of course! It all makes sense!" Mo said. Mo started running to the locker room to cure himself, but then turned around.

"By the way, you might not be cursed anymore, but you still need deodorant."

Kevin smacked himself on the head.

"I knew I was forgetting something."

Kevin was grateful the curse was gone and never uttered the name Sweaty Guy again.

KAZ

CHAPTER THREE

Kazoo Gremlin

Davy was supremely annoyed. His little brother Jacky had won a kazoo at the Slacksville Fall Festival and for two days had been humming every song he could think of into the kazoo at full volume.

Davy's dad put in earplugs and ignored Jacky.

Davy's mom asked Jacky to take breaks and would sometimes drown the kazoo out with the radio playing even louder in the kitchen.

Davy attempted to take the kazoo and smash it under his shoe, but when Jacky cried, his mom made him give the kazoo back *and* play horsey with Jacky for five minutes.

When they were done with horsey, Davy had a different idea.

"You got that kazoo two days ago, right? That's too bad. That means the kazoo gremlin will be here tonight."

"What's that?" Jacky asked.

"You didn't know? All the kazoos in the world belong to kazoo gremlins. The people at the carnival know this. They let kids believe they are winning kazoos, but really, they are just borrowing them. Then, after two days, the gremlins come looking for them. The best thing you can do is leave it on the front porch tonight. That way the gremlin won't have to come into your bedroom looking for it."

"But I don't want to give it back. I spent my allowance on tickets to play the balloon popping game and I *won* the kazoo. It's *mine*."

"Well, when the gremlin shows up in your room tonight, you better hope he's not angry. Or you could just play it safe and leave it on the porch. Your choice."

Jacky squinted at his kazoo like he was thinking about what to do.

That night Davy listened while his mom put Jacky to bed. He volunteered to take out the trash and planned to snag the kazoo off the porch on his way to the garbage can.

The problem was, the kazoo wasn't on the porch.

Davy sighed. Now he had to finish taking the trash all the way to the side of the house for what —Nothing!

He waited for his parents to fall asleep before he snuck into Jacky's room to look for the kazoo. He slowly opened the door and crept forward. Davy began touching objects on the dresser and felt his way through socks, a comb, loose change, and toys until...he felt the kazoo.

In the dark, a grin spread across Davy's face. But then that grin disappeared when he felt a rope grip his ankle and lift him into the air until his body was hanging upside down from the hook where Jacky's climbing rope normally was.

Davy cried out.

Jacky flipped on a flashlight and shined it on his own face.

"My parents won't hear you," Jacky said, "They fell asleep listening to whale sounds."

"Jacky, it's me!" Davy said, "What'd you booby trap your room for?"

"Clever little kazoo gremlin. Davy didn't mention you could disguise yourself, but one thing gave your real identity away—you smell much worse than Davy. You smell like the inside of a broccoli."

Davy sniffed at his armpit. *Did he really smell that bad?*

"Jacky, I made the gremlin thing up! I was just tired of hearing you play it and I wanted to get rid of it. Now let me down!"

Jacky was unmoved. There would be no convincing him.

"I'll let you down after we cut a deal. You leave the kazoo and never come back. Never! And tell your little gremlin friends to stay away too. And the tooth fairy! I don't trust anyone who collects teeth."

"OK, fine, I'll leave the kazoo and never come back," Davy said.

Jacky untied the knot in his rope and lowered Davy to the ground. He got back in bed.

"Leave the kazoo and close the door on your way out," Jacky said.

Davy pretended to put the kazoo back on the dresser, but slipped it into his pocket instead.

In his room, Davy tossed the kazoo into a drawer. He felt that Jacky still deserved to have the kazoo taken away after putting him in that trap.

He got under his blanket and waited for sleep. Just as he was beginning to drift off, he heard his door creak open.

"Go back to bed, Jacky," Davy said with his eyes still closed.

Then he heard quick steps across the floor. Something about it didn't seem right.

"Fiddle-ee-dee, fiddle-ee-doo! I have come for my kazoo!"

The door closed quickly and Davy flipped the light on with his heart racing.

The kazoo was gone.

CHAPTER FOUR

The Next Thing You'll Eat

Pippy and Davy walked into Pippy's house and dropped their bags by the front door.

"I have to show you something," Pippy said.

She led him over to her computer.

"I heard about this really weird website that tells you the next thing you're going to eat and I heard that it's always right. Isn't that crazy?" she said.

"There's no way it can always be right," Davy said.

"OK, here it is. I just have to put in my name and birth date."

Pippy typed her information in and pressed Enter.

"*Peanut butter filled pretzels.* That's impossible. Those are my favorite snack right now, but we ran out."

Just then, the front door opened and Pippy's mom came in with bags of groceries. Pippy and Davy gave each other a knowing glance.

"Mom. You didn't happen to buy peanut butter filled pretzels, did you?" she asked.

"I sure did. You want them?"

Pippy squealed in excitement.

"It worked!" she said. She ripped open the bag and started eating.

"My turn," Davy said.

He typed in his name and birthday.

"*Cockroach?!*" Davy shouted, "I'm not eating a cockroach! No way!"

Pippy explained the website to her mom who was in the middle of eating a piece of cheddar cheese.

"Type my name in," she said.

Pippy typed in her mother's name and birthday.

"*Cheddar cheese*. Amazing!" she said, and took another bite.

"Give me one of those things," Davy said, "I'll prove it's not true."

He grabbed the bag of peanut butter filled pretzels out of Pippy's hand, but first checked the ingredients.

"Contains milk. Darn. I can't eat it. I'm allergic to milk," Davy said.

Davy ran to the kitchen. He opened the snack cabinet and a cockroach scuttled out of sight.

"No!" Davy said, "I'm not eating a cockroach!"

Davy ran out of the house and all the way home. As soon as he got inside, he opened the pantry.

"No snacks," his mom said, "I don't want you spoiling your dinner."

"What's for dinner?"

"Burgers and salad."

Davy was relieved she didn't say *cockroaches.*

He nervously awaited dinner with his mouth shut. He didn't want any cockroaches to accidentally run into his mouth.

Finally, it was dinner time. He wasn't allowed to eat until someone said grace. It was their family tradition.

"Let me say grace tonight!" Davy said.

His parents gave each other a strange look.

"Go for it," his dad said.

"Dear God, please don't let me eat any cockroaches. Thank you for hamburgers. I'm not really thankful for salad, but thanks for salads, I guess. Amen."

Davy grabbed the ketchup and poured some onto his burger.

"You know, it's funny you should mention cockroaches," his dad said, "Did you know that meat processing plants are dirty places? There very well could have been cockroaches wherever this beef came from. The cockroaches could easily have fallen into the meat grinder. I could be about to eat some cockroach right now."

Davy froze and watched his parents take their first bites.

"We should really consider eating less meat," his dad continued, "But that still wouldn't save us from eating something like dead cockroach parts or maybe even mouse poo. Did you know that processed foods like ketchup or even the buns we're eating are *allowed* to have small amounts of insects or rodent hair in them?"

Davy set his burger down.

"Maybe I'll just eat the salad," he said. "The salad just came from a farm. It wasn't in some dirty factory, right?"

"That's true," his mom said, "But there could always be cockroaches in the grocery store just running around on the carrots at night. Who knows?"

She took a bite of her salad.

"The thing is, you just can't think about it or worry about it," she said.

Davy set down his fork. He was so hungry, but he didn't want that website to be right.

"Is there any food at all in this house that it would be impossible to have cockroaches in?" Davy asked.

"In theory, no. It's not likely, but there could be little bits of cockroach everywhere."

Davy turned green.

"Now eat before it gets cold," his mom said.

Davy's eyes felt wet. His stomach turned. He picked up his burger and took a bite.

It tasted good. And could something with cockroaches in it taste that good?

Davy felt relieved until he began to chew. He was quite sure he felt something different. Something that shouldn't be in a hamburger.

CRUNCH!

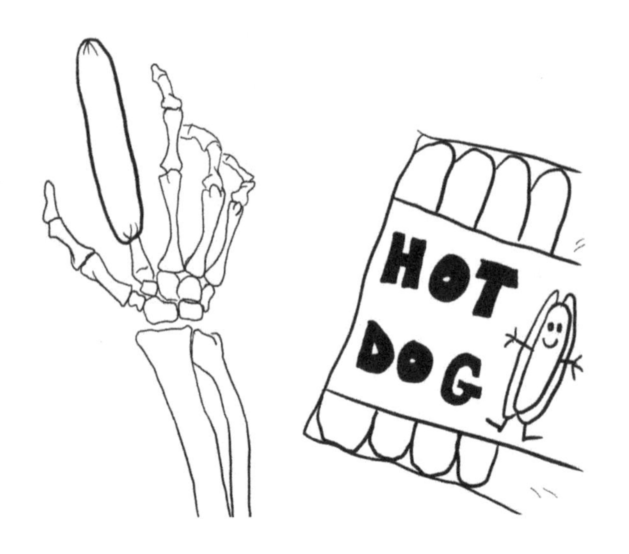
HOT
DOG

CHAPTER FIVE

Campfire Stories

Charlie's sister, Beatrix, glared at him over the campfire and took another bite of her hot dog bun covered in ketchup.

Charlie had accidentally dropped the entire pack of hot dogs into the fire when he tried to toss it to his dad. His dad fished the pack out of the fire with a stick, but the plastic was all melty on the hot dogs, so all they had to eat was buns and ketchup.

"It was an accident," Charlie complained to his sister again.

"We know it was an accident," his dad said, "But even when it's an accident, people are still allowed to have feelings about it. It'll be OK, buddy."

Charlie grumped and took a bite of his bun. He hated feeling like people were mad at him. This campout was turning out to be no fun.

Charlie's parents walked away from the campfire

leaving Charlie alone with his older sisters, Alice and Beatrix, and older brother Theo.

"I know!" Charlie said, "We should tell scary stories!"

After a moment of silence, Alice, spoke.

"You want a scary story? I'll give you a scary story."

Finger to the Bone

There once was a boy who had a mother who worked very hard. All day long she would do laundry, go to work, cook meals, vacuum the couches.

"You kids are going to work my fingers to the bone!" she would say.

The only good part of her day was that after her kids went to bed, she would do a crossword puzzle. While she worked the puzzle, she would drum her four fingers on the kitchen counter.

Thump-thump-thump-thump. Thump-thump-thump-thump.

The boy could hear the thumping from his bed where he was still awake. One night he finally called out. "Mom! Stop that thumping, I'm trying to sleep!" he yelled.

The mother sighed. All day long she had worked and just wanted 20 minutes of peace. If she wanted to thump her fingers, she would thump her fingers.

As the kids grew up, they got messier and messier, so the mother had to work harder and harder. As she used her hands, the skin on her fingers grew thinner and thinner and as the skin grew thinner, she started to go mad.

"You children! You're going to work my fingers to the bone!" she screamed.

More than ever, she couldn't wait until 8 PM when she could do her crossword puzzle.

One night the boy heard *click-click-click-click* from his bedroom. It was a sound he had never heard before. He thought of calling out to his mother, but instead got out of bed to see what the sound was.

He crept up silently behind his mother who was hunched over the dining room table with her crossword puzzle. The *click-click-click-click* continued.

"Mom?"

The clicking stopped.

She whipped around suddenly, pointed a bone finger at her son and cried, "What are you doing out of bed?!"

The boy screamed.

All of her fingers had no skin. She had literally worked all of her fingers to the bone and that was what made the clicking sound. She was drumming the bones across the table.

"S-sorry," the boy whimpered.

The mother turned back to her crossword, but from his bed he could still hear *click-click-click-click* and would have nightmares about the day his mother's hands turned to bones. She did give really good back scratches, but it was still spooky.

. . .

Charlie gulped.

"Alice?" he asked, "Was that story about *our* mom?"

"Of course not, it was just a story," she said.

But Charlie wasn't so sure.

"Does anyone else have a story?"

"I'll tell a story," Theo said.

The Mad Mower

Once there was a little boy who loved to ride his bike, but he could never remember to close the garage door.

He came home and his dad said, "Son, you forgot to close the garage door."

The boy said, "OK dad, I'll remember next time."

The next time he forgot again, and his dad said, "Son, you forgot to close the garage door, and now I'm going to take your bike away for one day as a punishment."

The boy said, "That's not fair. It was an accident. You can't punish me for making a mistake."

And the dad said, "There are still consequences for accidents. No bike tomorrow."

The next day, the boy decided that he didn't care what his dad said. He was determined to take out his bike. He opened the garage door and rode away. He didn't have any fun though, because he was nervous about what would happen when he got back.

While he was away, a bad guy came into the garage and stole the lawn mower. He was running around the neighborhood mowing all over the place. The boy froze at the end of his driveway, shocked at the sight of The Mad Mower, and saw his dad standing in the garage.

"Son!" he called out, "While you were disobeying me, that bad guy stole our lawn mower. You have about five seconds to get inside or else no screens for a week!"

And with that, the dad pushed the button to lower the garage door. The boy abandoned his bike and made a run for the door. As it lowered he began to crouch down, trying to decide if he could make it under. When he was a foot away he dropped to the ground and rolled under the door into the garage.

"I made it," he said to his dad, panting.

"Yeah, but look at your bike," his dad said.

The boy jumped up and looked out the window. The Mad Mower was running over the boy's bike, shredding it into a million pieces.

"Are you still mad, Theo?" Charlie asked.

"You mean about the time you left my bike in the driveway and Dad ran over it? No, I'm not still mad. You spent your whole allowance helping to buy me a new bike, remember?"

But Charlie wasn't so sure.

"Those stories were spooky. Maybe we should go to bed," he said.

"No!" Beatrix said as she licked the ketchup from her fingers.

"It's my turn to tell a story!"

The Dumb, Dumb Brother

There was a brother named Carl. Every day he messed up his sister's stuff. He spilled juice on her white sweater. He tracked dirt into her bedroom to borrow her tablet without asking. He knocked her toothbrush into the toilet.

The sister had enough. One day, she opened his sock drawer, glued eyes onto all the socks, and placed a curse on the drawer that turned all of the socks into sock puppets. Whenever he left socks on the floor, the socks would cry until he put them away. All day long he had to listen to the socks mumbling from inside his shoes that they couldn't breathe. One day, the socks had enough.

Carl dropped Flaming Hot Munchos on the floor and walked over them and the Flaming Hot dust got into his socks. He merely took the socks off and left them on the floor of his room.

That night, he woke up to a whimpering sound, looked down and saw a sock at the foot of his bed.

"Why do you leave me on the floor?" the sock said.

It inched halfway up his body like a worm.

"Why do you stuff me into smelly shoes?" the sock said.

It inched up to the boy's neck.

"Why did you put Flaming Hot dust on me?!"

And with that, all the socks in the sock drawer sprang into action. They completely covered Carl and no one knows what happened to him after that. Some people say he turned into a pile of socks. Anyway, at least he wasn't around to mess up his sister's things anymore.

Charlie shivered as his parents returned to the fire.

"I feel like everyone is still mad," Charlie said.

"Oh, honey," his mom said, "We're not mad. This is all just going to be a funny memory."

"And look! The camp store had hot dogs," Charlie's dad said.

Charlie's siblings brightened, but Charlie looked worried.

"What's wrong?" his mom asked.

"Everyone told some really scary stories while you were gone."

"Oh, but they're just stories. They're not real," his mom said as she took off her glove so she could stroke his face. Charlie was horrified to see that she was stroking his cheek with bony, skinless fingers. "All just stories."

Charlie's horror turned to laughter when she

skewered a hot dog on each finger and held it over the fire.

"Look! I'm Hot Dog Fingers!" she said, shaking the hot dogs above the flames.

Charlie giggled. She was right. It would all just be a funny memory.

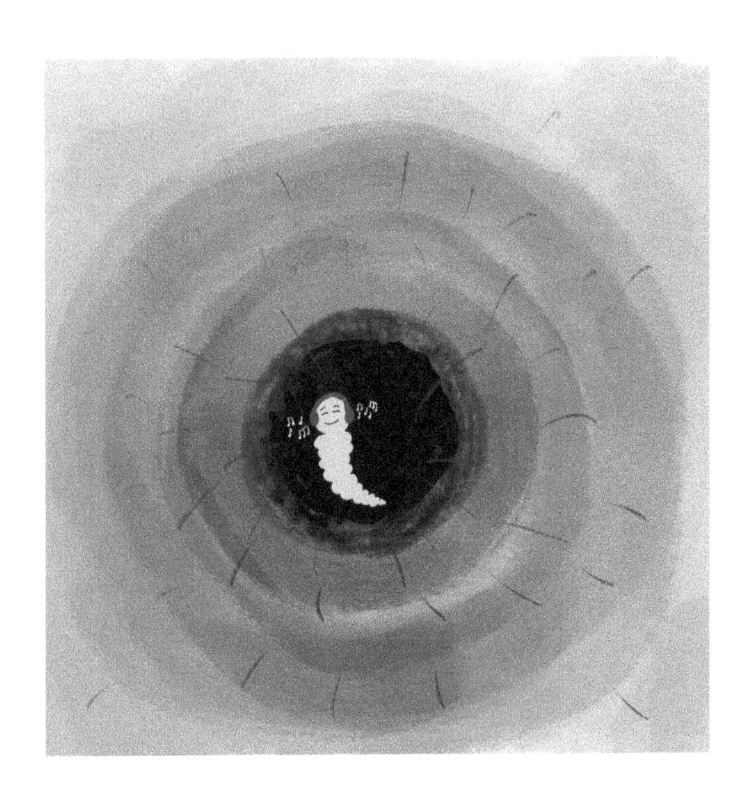

CHAPTER SIX

The Earworm

"I want to live inside your ears," Dawn sang.

"Live inside your ears," Kim sang, imitating the deep voice of Johnn-ay in *2 Slick 2 Slip*.

"So you can always hear me say," Dawn sang again.

The two girls each held a pen up to their mouths and sang together in the yard of Smirk Middle School.

"You're special! You're special! Especially Special! And I'd crawl past your ear wax! So I could beat it on your eardrum with the beat of your heart!"

The two girls fell into giggles.

"Is Johnn-ay still your favorite?" Dawn asked.

"Yes! Have you seen his new hair color? It's magenta!"

Mr. Miller stopped in front of them. He was monitoring their recess and was on his way to stop kids from picking Slacksville's famous glow-in-the-dark mushrooms, but he had to stop when he heard that song.

"I feel like I know that from somewhere," he said.

"It's the new *2 Slick 2 Slip* song. It just came out yesterday," Dawn said.

"Sounds like a real earworm," Mr. Miller said.

"What's an earworm?" Kim asked.

"A song that you just can't get out of your head. Almost like there's a worm living in your ear singing it to you constantly. Like a parasite."

"We don't care if it gets stuck in our heads," Dawn said.

Dawn and Kim kept singing.

When Mr. Miller arrived at the patch of mushrooms that had sprung up, he heard someone else humming the song.

"Kids, you know you're not supposed to pick mushrooms on government property. They make Slacksville especially special and when you pick them–"

"*No one else gets to enjoy them,*" the kids recited in unison. They had heard it a thousand times, but they liked rubbing the mushrooms on their arms. It left glow-in-the-dark spores on their skin.

"My mushroom smells like strawberry!" Sharla said, sniffing her arm, "I wish it *tasted* like strawberry."

The mushrooms may have had unique smells, but they still all tasted like mushrooms.

Again, Mr. Miller heard someone singing "*I'd die if I had to leave your ear canal, so let me whisper in your ear!*"

Such strange lyrics, Mr. Miller thought. *Almost like the song was about a* ***real*** *earworm.*

Mr. Miller saw to it that the kids stopped picking mushrooms and returned to his classroom for the rest of recess.

"*You're special, especially special!*" Mr. Miller muttered to himself, then he slapped himself across the face.

"I feel like I just need to hear the whole song, then I can get it out of my head," he said to himself. He put in earbuds and plugged into his computer. The song wasn't hard to find.

Mr. Miller recognized the lyrics he had heard the kids singing outside. He had to admit that the song was catchy, but for some reason he felt a little itch in his ear.

Even if you asked
I wouldn't be able to go
Like a sweet parasite
I need you to live
Like really, I'd die if I had to leave your ear canal
So please let me whisper in your ear
You're special
For eternit-ay

The itch in Mr. Miller's ear turned into a tickle. He wasn't sure if he could stand it.

The song wasn't quite over, but the tickle was too much. He just had to scratch the inside of his ear. He pulled the earbud away from his right ear, but it resisted–almost like a wad of gum was stretching between his ear canal and the earbud.

He kept pulling firmly until finally the connection, whatever it was, snapped.

Mr. Miller was horrified to see a short, juicy worm wriggle itself free from the inside of the earbud. It was pale white and had pincers at its front end and grubby legs on its sides. It rushed in little circles like it was panicked. Mr. Miller tried to slap his hand down on top of the worm, but it jumped up into the air and landed on his arm. He jumped out of his chair and wildly hopped from foot to foot while batting at his arm.

"Where is it?! Get it off!" he cried.

The earworm tickled his neck, ran up his jaw and into his ear. He tried to grab its tail end, but it was too late. He knew that sticking his finger in his ear would only push it further in.

"Calm down," he said to himself through panicked, heaving breaths.

Once he was quiet, he heard music. He shut off his computer, but the music still came.

If I'm stuck in your head
Don't see a doctor
Just listen to this song
For your happily ever after

Before he could think of what to do, his students began returning to the classroom. Had the bell rang? All he could think of was the song.

"Students," he said, straining to think, "We're going to begin our unit on, special...ear..."

He erased the lesson from the white board and started over.

"Let's take the day off from school work and learn all the lyrics to *2 Slick's* new song! Doesn't that sound fun?"

"Yeah!" they all agreed.

His ear no longer itched or tickled. It felt normal. The song was stuck in his head, but he liked it. Why would someone want to stop thinking about *2 Slick 2 Slip*? Grundy was most people's favorite, but he was more of a Johnn-ay guy. Yeah. Johnn-ay was the shy one.

"From the top! And-a One! And-a Two! And-a One, Two, Three, Four!"

"Listen, girl, I need you to hear what I say
You're especially special in your own special way
You're warm and fuzzy, so cute and fun-ay
But most of all I like when you listen to ma-ay!"

CHAPTER SEVEN

The Double

"Wesley! It's time to get ready for bed!"

Wesley rolled his eyes. He was in the middle of playing *Yeti, Set, Go!* and he was about to melt the Snow King. Unfortunately, his heat-ray ran out of power and he lost. Again.

"I'm in your bathroom waiting for you!" his mother called.

She was a stickler about brushing his teeth.

Wesley shut the TV off and lumbered out of the living room and into the hallway. He nearly yelped when a hand darted out of the coat closet and yanked him inside, but he couldn't make a sound because another hand came around his mouth.

"Shhhh. It's me," Wesley's mom said.

She let her hand off of his mouth. Wesley's heart began to beat fast. He reached for the light switch in the dark coat closet. His mother swiped his hand away.

"No!" she whispered. "She'll see the light under the door!"

"Mommy? What's happening?" Wesley whimpered.

"I heard the voice too," she said.

Once again, Wesley heard his mother's voice calling from the bathroom.

"Wesley, turn off the game and come to the bathroom. I'm waiting!" she called.

Wesley's eyes adjusted to the darkness and he could see his mother's eyes, her hair, and her pink bathrobe.

"Just stay quiet!" his mother whispered next to him in the closet.

The mother from the bathroom stepped into the hall. They could see her shadow beneath the closet door.

"Are you playing hide-and-seek with me?" She called out, "Ready or not, here I come!"

Wesley's mother who had been calling for him whipped open the closet door and screamed.

Wesley's mother from the closet screamed.

Wesley screamed.

His bathroom mother pulled him away from his closet mother.

"Who are you?!" she shouted.

Wesley looked into his mother's eyes in the hallway and wondered how he could ever possibly know which mother was real.

He looked back at the closet mother and saw that

they had the same eyes, the same body, the same expression of horror on their faces...

There was one difference, though.

The mother in the closet had a bushy, brown mustache.

"Honey, I know you must be confused. I am too! But you have to believe me! I'm your real mother!" the one with the mustache shouted.

Wesley and his actual mother looked at each other.

"Uhhhhh...obviously you're not," Wesley said.

"What are you, like a boogie man or something?" Wesley's mother asked the woman in the closet.

"No! I'm..."

The woman in the closet touched her face and felt the bushy mustache. She stopped pretending to be horrified and relaxed.

"Shoot! I didn't transform all the way. OK, you guys got me! I *am* the boogie man!"

Wesley and his mother laughed.

"Nice try, boogie man," Wesley said.

"OK, Wesley's getting ready for bed, so, time to go," his mom said.

The boogie man stepped out of the closet, walked into Wesley's bedroom, laid down on the floor and rolled under his bed. Wesley's mother lifted the side of the blanket to check if the boogie man was gone. There was nothing under the bed but a few forgotten socks and comic books.

Wesley tried to get under the covers, but a hand grabbed onto his ankle!

It was his mother pulling him back out of bed.

"Boogie man or not, you still have to brush your teeth, mister!"

500,000

CHAPTER EIGHT

The First Sleepover

Gavin did not want to go to his first sleepover. If it had been at his best buddy's house or even at his cousin's, he would have been excited, but instead it was some kid he had never even heard of before.

"Whose house am I sleeping at?" he asked, screwing up his face.

"My best friend's friend's son. His name is King. He's new in town and doesn't know anyone."

"So, why do *I* have to roll out the red carpet? I mean, if he was going to my school, I'd invite him to sit with me at lunch or play ball at recess. A sleepover, though?"

Gavin slumped over his peanut butter sandwich and felt a little knot in his stomach. He didn't want to go to a strange house.

His mom sat down across from him with her coffee.

"Let's go over a few rules. Rule number one–if

their house is a little different from ours, remember that that's OK. As long as it's safe, there's nothing wrong with it looking a little different."

Gavin thought back to the first time he went to Luke's house. It was smaller than theirs, but Luke had his own room in the basement. That was pretty cool.

"Rule number two," she said, "be polite if they have food that is unfamiliar to you. Whatever it is, give it at least one bite."

Gavin didn't like this rule, but wondered if King's family might be the kind of family that eats dessert every night. He could only hope.

"Rule number three–be flexible."

Being flexible usually meant being a good sport about doing stuff he didn't enjoy. Gavin didn't care for this rule either.

"Finally, rule number four–if you feel uncomfortable about anything at any time, you can call me and I'll come get you right away. Don't do anything you aren't comfortable with. This rule is more important than any of the other rules."

Rule number four made Gavin feel much better. He figured he'd stay a little bit, see what kind of video games they have and then call his mom to tell her he had a tummy ache or something. Easy peasy.

"Alright. I'll pack my bag," he said.

On the drive over, Gavin worried, but every time he worried he remembered that he could always call his mom.

The drive took them all the way to a new housing development with a sign that read TROUSER GREEN, but the neighborhood was hardly green. It was muddy, had construction trucks and only one house.

His mom pulled into the empty driveway. The house was dark.

"Are you sure they're even home?" Gavin asked.

"Sure I am!" she said. "And don't forget–call me when you feel done."

Gavin patted his pocket and felt his cheap little phone with no apps. The phone was just to call his parents.

He grabbed his bag and walked up to the house alone. He couldn't believe that his mom drove away before he even went inside.

"Weird," he said.

The doorbell was one of those doorbells that was also a camera. He pressed the button and–to his surprise–it didn't make a *ding dong* sound. The button made the door pop open.

"Umm...hello?" Gavin called out.

It began to rain, so he quickly stepped inside. When he looked back, he noticed that the street looked dry while the area in front of the door was soaking wet.

"Well, guess the rain has to start somewhere," Gavin said to himself. He closed the door before the rain could blow into the house. To his surprise again, there seemed to be nobody home. As for the house, there was a long hallway going both directions and in front of him, a TV screen.

"Hello? King?" he called out.

The TV screen came to life and the speakers blared out cheesy game show music. A big face appeared on the screen. It was a man wearing a crown and a huge grin.

"*Welcome, Gavin, to Sleepover Adventure! The game where kids have a chance to win FIVE HUNDRED THOUSAND CENTS!*"

Gavin's heart began to race. That was a lot of money, but he had never even heard of this game show. He had no idea what was going to happen next.

How do I play? Gavin wondered, *Does my mom know about this?*

"*I know what you must be asking yourself,*" King continued, "*How do I play and does my mom even know this is happening? I can answer both questions at once. Your mom told you the rules before you got here! Good luck!*"

The TV turned off.

"Huh?" Gavin said to no one. He racked his brain trying to remember the rules. Then he remembered the phone in his pocket. That was rule number four! He could call his mom any time he wanted to go home.

And what was the first rule? **It's OK if the house is different.** Not much of a rule, but Gavin figured it must be OK to go exploring. He kept his bag on his back and decided to walk left. When he looked up, he noticed cameras mounted high up on the walls. They turned to follow him. At the end of the long white hallway, he had two directions to choose from–two more long hallways.

"How do I know which way to go?" he asked.

No one answered the question, but talking things out always helped him think.

"They look almost the same, but the rugs are different. That hallway has a green rug. The other one has a red rug. I'll take the one with the green rug."

Gavin kept walking and found that every time he turned a corner, he had to choose between a hallway with a green rug and one with a red rug. He felt quite smart until he came to the choice between a purple rug and a blue rug.

"What do I do now?" he asked.

Each hallway had a door at the end.

"I guess it's my choice," he said. "Blue is my favorite color. I'll bet my mom told them that. So maybe they're trying to trick me into choosing that direction."

Gavin chose the hall with the purple rug and opened the door at the end. When he walked through, he found a dining room. There was a fancy silver dome with a fork and knife next to it.

"Rule number two. **Be polite if the food is not familiar. Try at least one bite.**"

When Gavin walked closer to the table, he found a note.

We made your favorites! it said.

Gavin lifted the lid and was confused. It was a big dish of brown mush. It didn't smell very good.

"This isn't my favorite. What is it?" Gavin asked.

He looked closer and saw a tiny bit of pepperoni. Next to it, there was a little melty puddle of chocolate ice cream. He saw shreds of cheddar cheese, crumbles of peanut butter cups, a smear of grape jelly, and mushed up french fries with ketchup. All of his favorite foods were all mixed together in one big disgusting pile.

"No fair!" he said. "It's not my favorite when it's like this!"

He knew what he had to do. He wasn't going to like it, but he had to take one bite. He worried that if the bite was too small, it wouldn't count, so he scooped up a big bite with the fork. He plugged his nose, chewed and swallowed the food down as fast as he could.

"Bleehhhh!"

He looked up at the camera and imagined people laughing at him.

There was another door and Gavin figured it was time to walk through it. He turned the doorknob and gasped at what he saw next.

It was a darkened room with red laser beams criss-crossing the room in all directions.

"**Be flexible,**" Gavin said. That was the third rule.

There was no chance he could jump and crawl

through this maze of lasers with his backpack, so he dropped it at his feet.

"Here we go," he said.

He stepped over the first laser beam and made twenty moves to get across the room. Sometimes he would have to duck under one and step over another at the same time. Toward the end, he rolled under a beam, stood up and laughed.

"I did it!" he shouted. There was one final door to walk through. He stepped out into the back yard of the house. He thought of the final rule.

"**Call Mom,**" he said. "Easy peasy!" Only he patted the pocket where his phone was supposed to be and found that it was empty. He turned back and just as the door was swinging shut, he saw that his phone was lying on the floor. It had fallen out when he rolled under the last laser beam!

"No!" He shouted, "My phone!"

The door closed and when Gavin tried to reopen it, it wouldn't budge.

By now it was dark. Gavin was standing alone, in the cold, in a neighborhood of Slacksville he didn't know.

"What do I do now?"

He started to panic.

"I need to call Mom. I'm definitely uncomfortable. I need to call Mom, but I have no phone and have no idea where to find one. Call Mom. Wait a second...*call* Mom!"

Gavin didn't need a phone to call his mom.

"Mooooooom!" he yelled.

"Gavin!" she yelled back.

The cheesy game show music began blaring all around him. His mom, Dad, his friend Luke, and that weird smiling game show host came running from around the corner with a whole camera crew and bright lights.

"You won!" The host said, "What are you going to do with all that money?"

Gavin thought for a moment.

"Buy this house!" he said. "This is the coolest house I've ever been in. One thing though..."

"What's that?" the host asked.

"This house needs better food."

CHAPTER NINE

The Wishing Washer

"Hey! We found it!" Jen said. She patted her pockets. "And once again, I don't have any change!"

"What is it?" Brian asked.

The two approached an old, rusty washing machine that someone had dumped in the middle of the Slacksville Forest.

"The Wishing Washer," she said. "I heard that if you throw a coin in and make a wish, the wish comes true. The first time I found it, I didn't have any change. I came back later with my mom's credit card thinking *that* would get me a really good wish, but it didn't work. And I couldn't get my mom's credit card back."

Brian peered into the washing machine. It seemed to be bottomless. He put his hands in his pockets and found nothing.

"Hey look! A roll of quarters!" Jen said.

She picked the quarters up off the ground and unraveled the paper.

"Why would someone leave a roll of quarters out here?" Brian asked.

"I don't know. Let's split them!"

An evil laugh echoed out from the washing machine.

"*Muah ah ah ah ha ha ha!*"

"What was that?" Brian asked.

"Who cares! Start wishing!"

Each of them held a handful of coins and grinned at one another. They started making wishes and threw a coin in for every wish.

"I wish we didn't have to go to school anymore!" Jen yelled.

"I wish my mom served ice cream for dinner every night!" Brian said.

"I wish I was good at basketball!"

"I wish I had my own personal robot butler!"

"I wish it was Christmas every day!"

On and on they went making wishes for toys and sugar and fun. Then the final wish.

"I wish that when we got back to town, everyone was a dog, but they could talk and wear clothes!" Brian yelled.

"Huh?" Jen asked. "That was a weird one."

Brian shrugged and smiled.

"Let's go!" he said.

On their walk back to their neighborhood, they

found a basketball in the street. Jen picked it up and swished the ball through a nearby hoop.

"Hey! The wish worked!" Jen said.

Brian cheered her on, but then suddenly scrunched up his nose.

"What's that smell?" Brian asked.

Jen sniffed the air.

"Smells like dog doo-doo."

They looked around for the source of the smell. As they kept walking, they started seeing piles of dog doo-doo everywhere. Brian accidentally stepped in some.

"No! I hate that smell!" Brian shouted, "I gotta get home and wash this off."

"See ya," Jen said.

While Brian was running home, he saw dogs out for walks on their own. They were wearing clothes too.

Did it actually work? Brian wondered

At his house, he turned on the hose and started spraying off his shoe.

"*May I help, master?*"

Brian's heart leaped. His own personal robot butler had snuck up behind him! And wanted to clean the doo-doo off his shoe!

"Yeah! Thanks, robot!"

Brian hopped into the house on one foot and found a strange dog in the kitchen. She looked like a border collie, but was wearing his mom's slacks and t-shirt.

"Brian!" she said, "What do you think of my new look?"

Brian's jaw dropped.

"Cool!" he said.

"I like it," she said. "You should see how fast I can run now."

"Can we play fetch after I finish my homework?" Brian asked.

"Sure, but there's no homework. School is canceled forever. We can play fetch after you have dinner. Oh, and Merry Christmas, by the way."

Brian's mom used her teeth to pull the lid off a container of ice cream. She used her paws to dig into the frozen treat, formed a glob of it and used her mouth to place it in a bowl.

"Here you go, sweetie."

She nudged the bowl across the floor with her nose and Brian picked it up. There was bits of dog fur in the ice cream and, although he couldn't see it, he just knew that his mom's dog spit was on it too.

"Uh, thanks," he said. He threw it away when she wasn't looking.

"Let's go play fetch," she said as her tail began wagging.

His mom *was* faster than ever and he thought it might be a good thing that she was a dog now. Then his dad arrived home from work, looking like a Scottish terrier, and his parents fought over a piece of rope. They even barked at other dog people that walked past the house.

When it began to get dark, Brian's dad nudged the house door open.

"Time to get to bed, son. You have a big day tomorrow."

"What do you mean? School got canceled. I don't have to do anything!"

"There was an emergency meeting at town hall about our new situation. The only people who aren't dogs are you and your friend Jen. We need the two of you to start picking up dog doo-doo. Nobody else has hands to do the job. Since you don't have school, it will be your career now."

"Yuck! No thanks!" Brian said.

"Sorry bud," his dad said. "It's not an option. We passed a new law that said you and Jen have to do it. Every day."

Brian ran into the house and started searching for coins.

"What are you doing?" his parents asked.

"I need coins! Now!" he said.

"It's the darndest thing, I *just* took all my coins to the bank a few days ago," his mother said.

Brian thought hard. There had to be coins somewhere. He ran to his room and opened the secret box he kept under his bed. He pushed away the paper money and Slacks cards. No coins.

He ran to the couch and overturned all the cushions. No coins.

The doorbell rang and Brian's robot butler answered it. It was Jen, out of breath from running.

"Brian, you have to undo the wish! They're going to make us pick up all the doo-doo!"

"I know! I need a coin!" he said.

Jen opened her hand. She had one coin.

Together they ran through the forest and found the Wishing Washer again.

"I wish..." Brian called out, "Wait, can I keep my robot butler?" he asked Jen.

"I don't know the rules," she said.

"I wish to undo all of our wishes–except the robot butler!"

He dropped the coin in.

They were tired, but it was already dark, so they ran back into town anyway. They were relieved to see that people were people, there were no Christmas decorations up, and Jen was bad at basketball again.

Brian's parents were waiting for him on his front porch.

"You can't just run off like that, mister. Now head to bed. Like I said, you have a lot of work to do tomorrow."

"What do you mean?" Brian asked. "Everything is back to normal."

"Well, the doo-doo didn't just disappear. You and Jen are going to have to take responsibility for it," his mom said, and then scratched her neck with her foot. "I'm still getting used to not being a dog."

The robot butler welcomed Brian home and offered him warm pajamas for bed.

"Robot butler? Could you plug my nose for me while I pick up all that doo-doo tomorrow?"

"*Yes, master,*" it said.

That was a relief. Still, Brian didn't think he'd be making any more wishes any time soon.

CHAPTER TEN

The Totally Non-Cursed Mummy

Ben and Luke were doing their usual thing on a summer day—walking around town. They didn't know where they were going or what they were doing, but they were never bored.

"We could go get ice cream?" Ben suggested.

Luke reached into his pocket and pulled out change.

"I only have fifty cents."

"Darn," Ben said.

Ben thought they might just wander around all day until he saw balloons floating above a sign.

"Yard sale!" Ben said, "Let's check it out."

The sale was in front of an old house. The light green paint was peeling from the siding and leaves filled the gutters. An old man sat in a chair on his driveway surrounded by tables full of trinkets. His gray hair seemed to fly away from the sides of his head and he wore a shabby brown sweater despite the hot day.

"What are–" the man started to say, but then his voice erupted into coughing. He cleared his throat. "What are you boys looking for today?"

"Nothing really. I only have fifty cents," Luke said.

"Well, it's just your luck," the old man said. "Everything costs fifty cents. Be careful what you choose, though. One of the items is cursed."

Ben and Luke smiled at each other.

"Whoa! Which thing is cursed?" Ben asked.

The old man crossed his fingers over his lips as though he was zipping them shut. The boys would just have to guess.

The items looked pretty ordinary. A box of fancy hankies. A hammer. A broken watch.

"Ooh, it has to be this!" Luke said, and he held up a doll with big eyes, messy hair, and a crack across its face.

"Nope," the man said.

Ben walked to another table. He saw a glass paperweight, a dusty old puzzle, and some fake flowers.

"Maybe this?" Ben said, and he held up an old mask that looked like a clown's face.

"Wrong again," the man said.

Both boys walked up the driveway, past a rusty tricycle, past a rocking chair that seemed to move on its own, all the way to a large box.

"We found it!" Luke said.

"Definitely, this is it!" Ben said.

The two boys worked together to hold up the dusty mummy they found inside. It looked just like all the pictures of mummies they had ever seen. It had tattered rags wrapped around every inch of its body, but it was lighter than they expected.

"Nope," the man said, "You two boys just don't recognize a cursed object when you see one."

They set the mummy back down and found a paper in its box with directions on how to bring it to life and how to make it rest again.

"Let's buy it!" Luke said.

"I'll say the magic spell so it can walk and we won't have to carry it," Ben said.

He said the magic words. The mummy sat up, grunted, and stood next to the boys. Luke handed the old man fifty cents and could've sworn he heard the old man quietly laugh.

"Let's go!" Luke said.

The mummy was a little stiff, but it ran behind the boys all the way to the ice cream shop.

"Mummy, can you buy us ice cream?" Ben asked.

The mummy pulled a wallet out of his bandages, peeked inside, and handed them a few dollars each. They all walked away with an ice cream cone. Seeing the mummy lick ice cream was kind of gross, but still very cool.

"Let's go to Sloth Park!" Luke said.

They ran to the park.

"Mummy, can you push us on the swings?" Ben asked.

The mummy pushed them on the swings and never seemed to get tired.

Meg and Lily walked past and stuck their tongues out at Luke.

"Mummy, can you give me advice about girls?" he asked.

The mummy patted him on the back and grunted.

"Yeah, that makes sense," Luke said.

After that, they rode bikes. Ben borrowed his dad's bike for the mummy. They found a hill to ride down over and over again. The mummy was starting to unravel a little.

"What happens when all the bandages fall off?" Luke asked Ben.

"I don't know. Do you think your parents will let you keep a mummy at home? Because mine definitely won't."

"Mine either. They won't even let me get a rat. Maybe we need to take him back."

Ben nodded in agreement.

They rode bikes back to the old man's house where they found him packing his leftover things into boxes. He didn't look surprised to see them.

"Hey mister, can we return the mummy?" Ben asked.

The old man began to laugh. He paused, then laughed some more. Then he coughed. Then he laughed again.

Ben and Luke weren't sure what to do.

The old man then pointed to a sign they didn't see earlier.

NO REFUNDS

He laughed even harder, but the boys were relieved.

"That's OK," Ben said. "We don't need a refund. We just want to return him."

"But you can't do that!" the old man said.

"Why not? The sign doesn't say NO RETURNS." Luke said.

"Darn!" the old man said, "Outsmarted by a couple of kids again!"

The boys said goodbye to the mummy, asked it to get back in its box, and said the magic words to put him back to rest.

The sun was low in the sky, which meant the boys needed to get home for dinner.

"Wait! Don't you want to know which item was cursed?" the old man asked.

Ben and Luke shrugged.

"I lied to you earlier. The doll is cursed. You were right all along."

"I knew it!" Luke said.

The old man didn't know it, but Ben had swiped a bandage off the mummy. The bandage was just long enough to make two friendship bracelets so they could both remember their wonderful day with the non-cursed mummy.

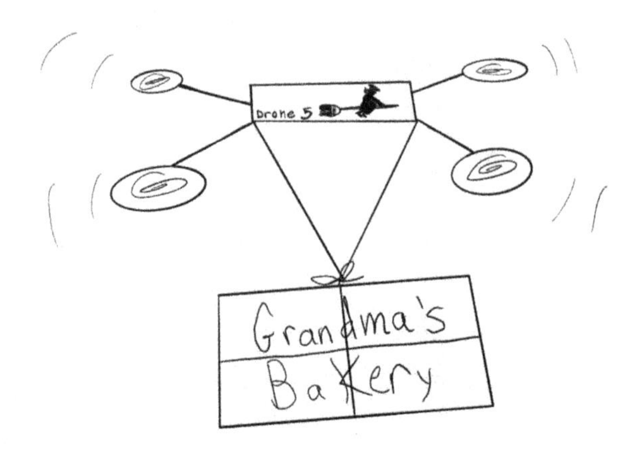
Drone 5
Grandma's
Bakery

CHAPTER ELEVEN

The Fairy Tale

Olly had an assignment from school and he thought the whole thing was dumb. The assignment was to rewrite a fairy tale.

"Fairy tales are kid stuff!" he said to his mom at dinner.

"Well, why don't you take a fairy tale and rewrite it so it's *not* kid stuff," his mom said.

Olly thought about it for a moment.

"Could it have fighting in it?"

"Sure," his mom said, "I don't see why not, as long as it's not too violent."

Olly speared a few green beans and shoveled them into his mouth.

"Could it be scary?"

"Sure. Lots of fairy tales are already scary, aren't they?" his mom asked.

Olly thought some more while he mixed his chicken with his mashed potatoes. *Yeah,* he thought, *some of them are kind of scary when you take away the cute parts.*

"Could I make it a movie instead of writing it?" he asked.

"That's up to you and your teacher," his mom said.

Olly already decided though, that it would have to be a movie if he was going to make it scary. The problem was, Olly didn't always plan ahead very well. He thought about the story of *Hansel and Gretel.*

He drew squares on a piece of paper, kind of like a comic book, and drew the opening scene in the upper left corner. It was a picture of breadcrumbs leading into a forest. The other squares were blank, but he decided that instead of planning ahead, he would just go start. He was too excited to figure the rest out.

On Saturday, Olly shoved a bag of bread and an old video camera he got from a thrift store into his backpack and rode his bike to the park, which was on the edge of Slacksville Forest. It was a little cold, so no one was around.

He created a trail of breadcrumbs, or rather, chunks of whole wheat bread, going into the woods. He started making his movie. He slowly walked over the trail of bread looking into the camera screen until something entered the shot that he hadn't put there.

It was a shoe.

Olly jumped back.

It wasn't just a shoe. The shoe was connected to a boy.

"You scared me," Olly said.

"Didn't mean to," the boy said. "Me and my sister were just walking around. We're visiting our grandma. And there's not much to do at her house except eat way too much sugar."

"That sounds awesome!" Olly said.

The sister stepped out from behind a tree.

"Our grandma is a baker. You wanna come see the house? It's not too far."

Olly couldn't remember ever seeing a house in these woods, so he was curious and followed them. After walking a couple of minutes, the smell of warm cinnamon filled the air. The grandma opened the front door and let loose a drone with a pink box dangling from the bottom.

"Cars can't get back here, so she delivers by drone," the boy said.

"You've made a friend!" the grandma said with a sweet smile.

"Come on!" the girl said.

The girl and boy both darted into the house and Olly couldn't resist the possibility of delicious treats inside. When he stepped in, there he saw a great wooden table full of pink frosted cookies, heart-shaped tarts, cinnamon buns, pies, and cakes.

"Hansel, offer the boy some samples. Gretel, ask him if he wants a glass of milk or tea to go with his food."

Olly's heart sank.

"Your names are...Hansel and Gretel?" Olly asked.

"Yeah, since our grandma is a baker, our mom

thought it was sort of funny to name us that. You want some tea or milk?" Gretel asked.

"Milk, I guess," Olly said.

He looked around the room more closely. There was a huge oven with an iron door and at least a dozen paintings of gingerbread houses hung on the walls.

Hansel handed Olly a plate with samplings of all the treats. Olly started to wonder if he really should have gone into the house of a stranger, even if he was invited by kids. Kids can be strangers too. Their clothes were old-fashioned. The boy wore suspenders and the girl wore a long skirt and an apron.

Despite his doubts, Olly took a bite of cinnamon roll and it was about the best thing he had ever tasted.

"Why do you guys dress like that?" he asked, then realized how rude it sounded.

"I know," Hansel said, "we're not exactly jeans and sneaker people. It's just our mom is really into fashion and she buys our clothes."

Olly watched Gretel reach into the oven to pull out a baking sheet. The grandma crept up behind her and put a hand on her back.

"Watch out! She's gonna push you in!" Olly shouted as he jumped up from his seat.

Hansel and Gretel stared at Olly while the grandma began to laugh.

"Just making sure she didn't get burned, dear," the grandma said.

The grandma pulled her scarf from her head revealing a pouf of messy gray hair. Then she took up a broom and held it at her side.

"She's a witch!" Olly shouted.

"I can't believe how rude he is," Gretel said to Hansel.

Olly felt bad. He figured his imagination had gone a bit wild.

"I'm sorry," Olly said. "It's just, this whole house reminds me of a fairy tale."

He bit into a cookie. It was so good, but he still felt like he shouldn't be there in a stranger's house with his parents having no idea where he really was.

"Thank you for the food," Olly said, "I should really be going. I have a school project to finish."

Olly tried to open the great wooden door, but it wouldn't budge. He jiggled the handle and began to panic. He was locked in!

"Tricky door," Hansel said, "I'll get it."

Hansel opened the door for him. After Olly stepped out, Hansel got ready to release another drone delivery.

"Hold on, sweetie," grandma said, "I want to deliver that one personally. It's for a friend."

The grandma gripped the box under one arm, put her broom between her legs and flew away.

Olly gasped.

"Oh, you were right about her being a witch," Hansel said.

"But the way you said it sounded mean," Gretel said.

Olly couldn't run away fast enough. He didn't care that he was being rude. He felt certain that if he stayed any longer, something bad might happen.

He went home and wrote down exactly what happened, then turned it in to his teacher and let her know that it wasn't a story. It really happened.

She wrote an F at the top.

"I won't tolerate lies," she said. "Either tell me the truth or accept your grade."

A buzzing sound came nearer and nearer. Olly thought it sounded familiar.

"Ooh! My cookies are here!" his teacher said.

A drone flew a pink box into the room and all the way to the teacher's desk.

"The witch made those!" Olly said.

"OK, Olly, you get an F."

No one ever believed Olly, but he didn't feel brave enough to go looking for proof. Olly never went into the woods again.

CHAPTER TWELVE

See You Later

"Hey, kid," the woman's voice said.

Lily looked around her front yard. She was alone and she wasn't sure where the voice was coming from.

"Pssst! I can hear you out there stomping around your yard. I'm down here in the storm drain!"

There were no cars coming, so Lily walked into the street and looked down at the drain. It had bars like a little jail and, to her surprise, a woman's face behind them.

"Hey, little girl. You got any snacks out there?"

Lily was puzzled.

"Why are you in the sewer?"

The woman smoothed her green hair away from her face.

"I live down here. My name's Tuna. Do you have any snacks?"

"Why is your hair green?" Lily asked.

"Gosh, you sure have a lot of questions. If only you had half as many snacks," Tuna grumped.

Lily got on her hands and knees so she could peer further into the sewer.

"It stinks down there. Do you have, like, a bed and a kitchen and everything?"

"No, ya weirdo, I live in the sewer, there's just water and yucky stuff and rats. I'm tired of eating rats. Do you have potato chips? Or a can of beans?"

Up close, Lily could see that Tuna had long, flowing hair and blue eyes.

"Why do you live down there?" Lily asked.

"I can only live in wet places. Now, how about you go into your kitchen and check if you have any peanut butter and jelly or maybe some grapes."

Lily began to wonder if she should be talking to a strange woman in a sewer, but seeing as how there were bars between them, the woman couldn't hurt her. Could she?

"Do you really eat rats?" Lily asked.

"Yeah. It's slim pickings down here. A girl's gotta eat."

"What else do you eat?" Lily asked.

"Almost anything! Now hurry up and go get me some grub!" Tuna shouted.

Tuna grabbed the bars and pushed her face toward Lily. With more light on her face, Lily could see that the woman had long, sharp teeth. The sight made Lily stumble backward.

"Oh no. I scared you. Sorry kid. I didn't mean to

scare you. It's just that I'm so hungry, I would eat the first thing I could get my hands on."

Tuna tightened her grip on the bars and, for the first time, Lily noticed that her nails looked awfully sharp and dirty.

Lily ran into the house and wondered what she should get for Tuna. She found a can of chili and didn't think anyone would miss it. She ran back into the street and handed the can to Tuna.

"You didn't open the can!" Tuna said.

"S-sorry, ma'am," Lily said, her voice shaking.

Tuna simply bit her teeth into the can and ripped the lid off. She slurped and guzzled the chili until there was nothing left except for a smear of red around her mouth. It almost looked like blood.

Half of Lily's brain told her to run away and never look back, but the other half was too curious for her own good.

"Do you feel better?" Lily asked.

Tuna belched.

"I'll go get more," Lily said.

She was back in a jiffy with a cup of chocolate pudding and, secretly, a flashlight. While Tuna was busy slurping up chocolate pudding, Lily shined the flashlight down into the sewer. She couldn't believe her eyes.

The lower half of Tuna's body looked like a fish.

"Wow! You're a mermaid!" Lily said.

"No duh," Tuna said, "I'm still hungry."

Lily felt less afraid. Mermaids aren't scary!

"Why are you in the sewer?"

"Back to the questions, huh?" Tuna asked. She backed away from the bars slightly. "Come closer and I'll tell you."

Lily crawled in as close as she could and leaned her face right up to the bars. She didn't even care that her clothes were getting dirty and her hair was dragging on the ground.

"I used to live in a beautiful mermaid village in the ocean," Tuna said sweetly. "Every day we played, sang, and danced. I had 20 sisters and brothers. Our house was made out of shells. Yeah. Shells and gold from sunken pirate treasure."

Tuna's hand slipped out of the sewer and closer to Lily.

"There was coral of every color. And it tasted like candy."

Tuna's hand was like a spider walking across the pavement closer to Lily's hair.

"All we had to do was reach out and GRAB IT!"

Tuna grabbed onto Lily's hair and yanked it closer. Lily's face was inches from Tuna's sharp teeth. Lily thought fast, grabbed the sharp edge of the chili can, swiped it against her own hair, and stumbled backward. Tuna was left with only a handful of Lily's cut hair.

Tuna laughed.

"You kids always fall for it. A mermaid village. Ha!"

"There's no mermaid village?" Lily asked.

"Nah. I'm just a regular old sewer mermaid. We end up in the sewer when someone flushes a baby mermaid down the toilet."

Lily was frightened, but relieved that the mermaid couldn't come out from the water. She swore to herself she would never talk to someone from the sewer again.

Lily's relief turned to disgust, however. Tuna, the horrific sewer mermaid, was indeed *very* hungry. Hungry enough to devour the handful of Lily's hair. Tuna let out another belch and swam away with a splash.

Lily was shaken and went inside to wash up. As she leaned over the sink to wash her hands, a voice echoed up from the drain.

"*See you late*r."

ACKNOWLEDGMENTS

This book couldn't exist without Jonathan Hooker who figures out the hard stuff.

Thanks to Stacie Gensic who understood the book and edited it.

Thanks Andrew Dieffenbach for the great cover art.

Thanks to Mom for reading to me.

Thanks to Miss Tanner for having us write so much in fourth grade and Mr. Mullen for having us write so much in sixth grade.

ABOUT THE AUTHOR

K. Peach is a writer in Portland, Oregon. She is also a former children's librarian, mother, wife, and ghost story enthusiast. She guards the only known portal to Slacksville, but suspects there may be another one. Possibly in Colorado.

Stay in touch! We'd love to see your art on Instagram. Don't forget to use #slacksfart (that's short for Slacksville fan art). While you're there, follow Tales_From_Slacksville .

COMING SOON

Keep an eye out for Slacksville's Worst Superheroes!

CPSIA information can be obtained
at www.ICGtesting.com
Printed in the USA
LVHW011658181122
733278LV00019B/1132